MW01045593

A SUMMER ROMANCE

SUSANNAH BRIN

Artesian Press

P.O. Box 355, Buena Park, CA 90621

Take Ten Books
Romance

Connie's Secret	1-58659-460-5
Cassette	1-58659-915-1
Bad Luck Boy	1-58659-458-3
Cassette	1-58659-916-X
Crystal's Chance	1-58659-459-1
Cassette	1-58659-917-8
A Summer Romance	**1-58659-140-1**
Cassette	**1-58659-918-6**
To Nicole with Love	1-58659-188-6
Cassette	1-58659-919-4

Other Take Ten Themes:

Mystery
Sports
Adventure
Chillers
Thrillers
Disaster
Horror
Fantasy

Project Editor: Dwayne Epstein
Assistant Editor: Molly Mraz
Illustrations: Fujiko
Graphic Design: Tony Amaro
©2003 Artesian Press

www.artesianpress.com

 ISBN 1-58659-140-1

Contents

Chapter 1 5

Chapter 2 10

Chapter 3 16

Chapter 4 22

Chapter 5 29

Chapter 6 36

Chapter 7 42

Chapter 8 48

Chapter 9 52

Chapter 10 56

Chapter 1

Janey Morgan walked along the ocean's edge. Thick, foamy seawater bubbled over her feet. After sitting with her friends in the hot August sun, the coolness of the water felt good on her skin. Overhead, sea gulls squawked as they glided in the sky.

Janey didn't look up. She stared down at the wet sand as she searched for shells and colored beach glass.

Not much to pick from at this beach, Janey thought. All she found was a mussel shell. She was disappointed.

A few feet away, she saw something. A pink-and-white piece of shell sparkled in the sun for a moment and then disappeared beneath a wave.

She hurried forward in the water and bent down toward the spot where the shell had shined.

As her fingers closed around the half-buried shell, someone yelled, "Watch out!"

It was too late. A runaway surfboard banged into her leg and knocked her off balance. She fell down in the ankle-deep water.

"Hey, I'm sorry."

Janey quickly got up. She paid no attention to the brown hand that reached down to help her. Her green eyes looked angry as she saw the surfboard lying on the sand.

"Aren't you supposed to have a safety strap on your board tied to your ankle?" she asked angrily. She turned and looked into the concerned face of a handsome, dark-haired young man. He wore a black rubber wet suit.

He pointed to a broken black cord around his ankle as a way to explain.

"I guess I need to buy a new one," he said. He grinned at Janey as if to apologize.

Janey rubbed her ankle. A big bruise was already beginning to show.

"Are you okay?" he asked.

"I'll live," she mumbled. She started to feel less angry. Then she remembered the shell. She frowned and stared at the water that was slowly going out to sea. The shell had disappeared.

"Did you lose something?" the young man asked.

"A shell. I was just going to pick it up when your board smashed into me. Now I'll never find it," she said.

Janey heard herself talking as if she lost a diamond. Then, realizing how silly she sounded, she blushed.

"I can help you look," he said.

Seeing the amused expression on his face, Janey felt herself getting angry again. "Forget it. It's not important."

First, he knocks me down, then he laughs at me, she thought. She turned and walked down the beach toward her friends.

He began to walk beside her. "Do all redheads have a temper like you?"

"I don't have a temper," Janey said quickly. She tried hard to ignore him.

"Look, we got off to a bad start. My name is Tim Cody. My friends just call me Cody. I'm going to be a senior at Venice High this fall," he said. He stepped around in front of her, forcing her to stop walking. He held out his hand for her to shake.

Janey stared at his hand, then at his face. He looked so sincere, she felt her anger disappear. She gently squeezed his hand. "I'm Janey Morgan, and I'm going to be a senior, too," she said. In almost a whisper, she added, "I go to Pali High."

Sometimes she was embarrassed to say she went to Pali High. Everyone

8

knew it was where all the rich kids went to school. She looked at Cody to see his reaction. He didn't seem to care. She smiled to herself. She was glad that it didn't seem to matter to him that she went to Pali High.

Cody looked into Janey's eyes. He grinned. "You want to go surfing?"

Janey blinked. She was surprised at the sudden warm feelings she felt. She shook her head. "I've got to go. My friends are waiting for me."

"Some other time," Cody said. He looked down the beach in the direction she was going. It was down toward the private beach of the Malibu Colony. He turned and walked off toward his surfboard.

Janey bit her lip and watched Cody. He walked back into the ocean carrying his board. She sighed to herself and walked back to the beach house.

Chapter 2

When Janey got back to the beach house, only her friend Ming Lu was still lying on the sand. "Where is everyone?" Janey asked. She sat down on her beach towel.

Ming put down the book she was reading. "Inside, ordering a pizza or something. Did you have a nice walk?"

Janey smiled thinking about Cody. "Actually, I did."

"Kyle was really annoyed that you left," Ming whispered. She looked back toward the modern glass-and-redwood beach house to see if anyone was coming.

"Why, because I got bored with all

the stuff he bragged about buying with his money?" Janey asked angrily. She picked up her suntan lotion and began to rub it on her body. Unlike her friend Ming, who had long black hair and darker skin, Janey's pale skin burned easily.

"Well, you could at least act like you're interested in some of his hobbies, Janey. Guys like that," Ming said.

Janey looked at her friend as if she was tired of the conversation. "Okay," she said. "I'll act like I care about his new motorcycle. Don't expect me to go for a ride, though. You know what a reckless driver Kyle is."

Ming shook her head, as though she didn't understand Janey sometimes. She leaned closer to Janey. "All I am saying is you're going to make him look for another girl if you're not careful."

"So what? There are other guys," Janey grinned. She thought about

Cody. She liked the way his face looked when he smiled.

"I can't believe you're talking like this," Ming said. "You've been wanting to date Kyle Anderson for more than a year. Now that he's interested, you act like it's no big deal."

Janey knew Ming was right. She had wanted to date Kyle for a long time. She was thrilled when he finally asked her out. Not only was he good looking, he was the most popular boy in school. *Am I being silly?* she thought. She realized she probably would never see Cody again.

"Hey, the pizzas are here," Kyle called out from the beach house patio.

Bobby Brown, Ming's boyfriend, appeared at the railing next to Kyle, eating a piece of pizza.

Janey turned around and smiled up at Kyle and Bobby. "Be there in a minute," she said.

"Better hurry up or Bobby will eat

it all," Kyle laughed. He gave his buddy a playful punch in the arm.

"He will, too!" Ming shouted. She jumped up from her towel and ran to the house.

Janey laughed as she followed Ming across the sand. Ming was very thin, but she could eat like a football player.

Bobby grinned as they stepped out onto the patio. His mouth was full of gooey pizza. "I don't think you girls want any of this. It's fattening."

"You should think about that yourself, Bobby. Your waist looks like you swallowed an inner tube," Janey teased. Her green eyes sparkled playfully.

Bobby looked surprised. He looked down at his bare belly hanging over the waist of his swim trunks. "Yeah, this summer has been good to me."

Ming picked up a large slice of pizza. "Maybe too good."

Kyle laughed and put his hands on

his own slim waist. "Leave him alone, you two. Bobby's a defensive linebacker. He needs to add a few pounds before the football season starts."

Ming and Janey looked at each other and smiled. Carrying her pizza and a soda to the railing, Janey stared at the ocean. In the distance, she could see a group of surfers. She wondered if Cody was one of them, waiting for the next good wave.

Janey glanced over at Kyle. He was also leaning on the railing. She couldn't help but compare him to Cody. Both boys were tall and slim. Kyle had short blond hair and blue eyes.

Cody looked totally different. He had black hair that was longer and dark eyes. She could not stop thinking about how he looked at her. It made her feel like she was the only girl in the world.

"What are you thinking about, Janey? You seem so far away," Kyle said. He reached out and touched her arm with his fingers.

Janey stepped away from him. She suddenly did not want him to touch her. "Nothing," she lied.

"Is something bothering you?" Kyle asked. His blue eyes showed concern.

Janey started to say, "No. I just wish . . ."

"Good," Kyle said without letting her finish her sentence. He turned toward Bobby, who was drinking a soda. "Let's take the new motorcycle out for a ride, buddy."

"All right!" Bobby said. He gave the glass table a thump with his hand.

"Count me out," Janey said.

"Oh, come on," Kyle begged. He had his puppy-dog look on his face.

Janey shook her head. "I've got to go." The last thing she wanted to do was ride on an expensive motorcycle. She didn't want to take the chance that Cody might see her.

Chapter 3

Janey drove her small car into the driveway and parked. As she walked to the front door, her sandals slapped against the hot tiles of the walkway. The late afternoon air was heavy with heat.

Janey dropped her keys on the hall table. She walked on through the house to the back patio. Seeing her six-year-old sister, Marci, in the pool, she called out, "Hey, Marci, where's Mom?"

"She went someplace with Daddy," Marci said. She gave Janey a big smile.

"Well, what are you doing in the pool? You know you're not supposed to go swimming alone," Janey said.

Marci made a face. "Betty is

watching me."

Janey looked around the yard. She didn't see Betty, the family's housekeeper.

Before Janey could say anything, Betty popped her head out the side door by the kitchen. "Janey, you're home. Good. Now you can watch Marci. I have to get dinner ready."

Janey nodded and headed straight for the pool. "Here I come!" she shouted. She took a flying leap into the pool. When she came up for air, Janey shot a mouthful of water at her little sister.

Marci laughed and splashed water with her hands. Janey splashed her back. Then Janey rolled on her back and floated to the deep end of the pool. She stared up at the sky and wondered what Cody was doing now.

"Let's race," Marci said. She began to swim up next to Janey.

Janey smiled at her little sister.

"Okay, but you know I'm going to win."

"Not if you let me go first," Marci said. She had a hopeful look on her face. Janey laughed and gave her a head start. They swam several lengths of the pool. Janey let Marci win every lap.

"That was fun!" Marci shouted. Her little face smiled with pleasure.

Janey laughed and pulled herself out of the pool. "Time to get out. Take a rest," she said. She knew her sister would stay in the water for hours if allowed. She picked up a fluffy white towel. When Marci climbed out of the pool, Janey wrapped the towel around her and gave her a hug.

Marci wiggled out of the hug and ran toward the house. Janey shook her head. Her little sister was so full of energy. Wrapping a towel around herself, Janey lay down on a lawn chair. She yawned and closed her eyes. She fell asleep thinking about Cody.

An hour later, Janey woke up just as her mother, Mrs. Morgan, came out of the house.

"Kyle is on the phone," her mom said. Her high-heeled shoes clicked on the concrete patio as she walked.

Janey got up and met her mother halfway. She took the phone and covered it with her hand. "Thanks, Mom."

Her mother smiled. She walked to the sunroom where Janey could see her father sitting. He was drinking iced tea.

"Hi," Janey said into the phone. She listened as Kyle asked her to go with him, Ming, and Bobby to a movie. She asked Kyle to wait. She called across the patio to ask her mother for permission. Her mother nodded.

"I can go," Janey said into the phone. "Eight o'clock? Okay, I'll be ready." She hung up the phone and walked toward her parents.

"Hey, honey, how are you doing?" asked her father. Mr. Morgan lifted his head and Janey gave him a kiss. Then, he smiled.

"I'm fine," Janey answered. She reached for a glass to pour herself some iced tea.

"Did you have fun today?" her mother asked. Her green eyes were the same color as Janey's.

Janey nodded. "I went out to Kyle's parents' beach house. Ming and Bobby were there, too. We sat on the beach and I took a walk." Janey didn't mention meeting Cody.

"I saw Kyle's mother today. She gets her hair done at the same place I do," Mrs. Morgan said. Her smooth-skinned hand touched the ends of her straight brown hair. Janey got her own reddish hair from her father.

"That's funny. I was at the studio today and saw Kyle's father," Mr. Morgan said.

Janey sipped her iced tea and remembered how Kyle liked to brag to his friends that he could introduce them to movie stars. She frowned because she really didn't care about that sort of thing.

She looked from her father to her mother. She thought for a moment that they were really good-looking people, for parents, anyway. "I'm going to go take a shower."

As Janey left the room, she heard her mother say what a fine boy Kyle was and how pleased she was that Janey was dating him. "His family is our kind of people," Mrs. Morgan said.

Disgusted, Janey knew what her mother meant. Kyle went to the same school, and his family had a lot of money. *So, how come I can't stop thinking about Cody?* she wondered.

Chapter 4

As Janey and Kyle walked out of the movie theater, she turned to him. "I'm going to the ladies room. I'll meet you out in front," she said.

"Yeah, no problem," Kyle answered. His attention turned to Bobby and Ming, who were a couple of steps behind him. "The special effects in the film were awesome. What did you think, Bobby?"

Janey signaled Ming where she was going. Ming walked to her side and together they walked away.

When they entered the ladies room, Janey stood in front of the mirror. She ran her hand through her short red hair, then put on some lip gloss.

"You really should darken your eyelashes," Ming said. She put a dark red lipstick on her lips. "Or wear eye shadow."

"I don't like fussing with all that stuff," Janey said. She leaned into the mirror and looked at her reflection.

Ming snapped her purse shut and put the strap over her shoulder. "Ready?"

Janey nodded and followed Ming out into the hallway. As they went past the people at the snack counter, Janey heard someone call her name. She turned and looked up into the smiling face of Tim Cody.

"Oh, hi," Janey said. She tried to keep the excitement of seeing him out of her voice. "What are you doing here?"

Cody grinned as though he thought it was a silly question. "I just saw *Endless Summer*, again. It's an old surfing film."

"We saw *Swamp Monsters*," Janey said. Hearing Ming clear her throat, Janey introduced her to Cody.

Ming smiled at Cody. "Nice to meet you," she said. She turned to Janey. "I'll be outside," she said.

Ming walked away before Janey could stop her. Janey was now alone with Cody. She knew she should go. Kyle and the others would be waiting. Still, she didn't want to leave.

"How's your leg, where my board hit it?" Cody asked.

Janey felt her cheeks get warm. "Just a bruise. It's nothing, really."

"You should come over to Santa Monica Beach tomorrow. There's a surfing contest. Starts about eight," Cody said.

"Are you going to be in the contest?" Janey asked. She was really happy that he wanted to see her again.

"Yeah. And I meant it today about surfing. Anytime you'd like to go . . ."

Cody stopping talking. He looked at someone behind her.

Janey turned just as Kyle put his hand on her shoulder. She stepped away from Kyle, forcing him to take his hand off her. "Well, I guess I have to go," she said.

"I don't think we've met. I'm Kyle Anderson, president of the senior class at Pali High School," Kyle said.

Cody grinned and looked at Kyle's expensive shirt, slacks, and short blond hair. "Tim Cody," he said. He put out his hand to shake.

Kyle just stared at Cody's hand. Finally, Cody dropped his hand to his side. He shrugged like it was no big deal. "See ya around, Janey Morgan," Cody said. He turned and joined the crowd of people leaving the lobby.

Janey walked angrily toward the exit. She pushed her way through the swinging doors. Kyle caught up with her and grabbed her hand. She pulled

Kyle caught up with Janey and grabbed her hand.
She pulled her hand away.

her hand away.

"So, what's going on?" asked Bobby. He grinned and swung Ming's hand back and forth.

"Nothing. Janey was just talking to some surfer dude," Kyle said. He reached into his pocket and pulled out the keys to his big black car.

Bobby made a face. "Surfers are all losers," he said. "No offense, Janey, seeing as how he's your friend."

Janey shook her head. She liked Bobby, but sometimes he could be kind of dumb.

After they all got into the car, Kyle backed it out and drove down the street. He looked at Janey. "So where did you meet this Tim Cody? He doesn't go to Pali, does he?" he asked.

"Actually, I met him today when I took a walk on the beach. He goes to Venice High," Janey said. She really didn't want to talk about Cody.

"Oh, yeah?" Kyle said. Venice High

was Pali High's biggest sports rival.

"I'd like to go home," Janey said. She rubbed the side of her head.

"It's early," Kyle said. "I thought we would get some ice cream."

"I could go for something to eat," Bobby said.

Kyle laughed. "Dude, you are always hungry." He gave Janey a big smile to include her in his joke.

"I've got a headache. I'm sorry, Kyle, but I really want to go home," Janey said. She prepared herself for the argument she knew was coming.

Kyle reached out and put his hand on hers. "Okay. No problem." He smiled at her. "Whatever you want, Janey."

Sometimes she didn't know what to think of Kyle. He could act like a jerk one minute and the next minute, he could be kind and caring. If she could just stop thinking about Cody, everything would be perfect.

Chapter 5

Janey was up very early the next morning. She put on her swimsuit and then pulled on a gray sweatshirt and shorts. She ran a comb through her hair and went downstairs. She saw her father reading the paper in the kitchen.

"You're up early for a summer morning, Janey," Mr. Morgan said. A cup of coffee and half-finished bowl of cereal sat on the table in front of him.

"It's eight o'clock. Not that early. Besides, I couldn't sleep," Janey said. She gave her father a kiss on his cheek.

"Something bothering you?" he asked.

Janey smiled and shook her head. She knew she couldn't tell her father that she met a new boy she couldn't stop thinking about. "I'll see you later," she said.

"Where are you going today?" her dad asked.

"I'm going to the beach for a run," Janey answered.

He picked up his newspaper. "Well, have fun, honey," he said.

Betty stood at the marble counter. She was writing out a grocery list. She looked up as Janey poured herself a glass of orange juice. "Would you like some eggs or something?" Betty asked.

Janey made a face. "No way. This juice is enough."

Betty frowned and shook her head. "You should eat breakfast. It is the most important meal of the day. You're getting too skinny."

Janey laughed. She grabbed a corn muffin from the plate on the counter. It was still warm from the oven. "I'll eat one of these just to make you happy, okay?"

Janey finished her muffin as she started her car. Carefully, she drove out onto the street.

Once she was on the highway to the beach, Janey rolled down her window and breathed in the smell of the ocean. She switched on the radio. An old Beach Boys tune was playing. She wondered if Cody liked the Beach Boys.

She pulled her car into the parking lot next to the Santa Monica Pier. She suddenly wondered if she should be here. She hardly knew Cody. She jumped out of the car before she changed her mind again.

Walking under the pier, she could see a group of surfers sitting in the sand with their boards. Another group was in the water paddling out past the waves. She didn't see Cody anywhere.

She suddenly felt as if she didn't belong there. She walked down to the wet sand, away from the groups sitting on the beach.

"Hey, Janey!" Cody shouted. Janey turned and saw him jogging toward her. She took a deep breath. Dressed in baggy orange swim trunks and wearing sunglasses, he looked completely relaxed. *He sure is handsome,* she thought.

"I'm glad you made it," Cody said. He stopped a few feet in front of her and grinned. "I haven't gone out yet, so you'll be able to see my first ride."

"Cool," Janey said. She felt the attraction between them. For a long moment, neither of them said anything. They simply stared into each other's eyes. When she felt her cheeks get red, she stopped staring.

"Come on, I'll introduce you to some of the other kids," Cody said.

Janey stared at the wet sand, then out toward the ocean. She wasn't sure she was ready to meet his friends.

Cody must have known what she

was thinking, because he laughed. "My friends don't bite, I promise," he teased. He grabbed her hand and led her back down the beach.

Janey spent the rest of the morning and afternoon with Cody and his friends. Everyone was very friendly. When Cody surfed, she watched and asked questions about what the judges looked for and how they scored the different rides.

Watching Cody surf, Janey found herself admiring his athletic ability. He made surfing look so easy, she was tempted to try it.

"That's it for today," Cody said. He dropped his board on the sand next to Janey. Cody grinned and pulled off his wet suit.

"I think I got a lot of good rides. They'll give me a high score, but I won't know until tomorrow. This is only the first day," he said.

"Oh," Janey said sadly. She was

Watching Cody surf, Janey found herself admiring his athletic ability.

hoping he would teach her how to surf.

"Why the sad face?" he asked. He sat down on the sand next to her.

"I, um, was thinking it would be fun to try surfing tomorrow," she said

Jumping up, Cody grabbed her hand and pulled her to her feet. "What's wrong with now?"

"But you've been surfing all day. Aren't you tired?" Janey asked. She started to pull away, but his hand held hers, strong and firm.

"I never get tired of riding waves," Cody said. "Come on." With his free hand, he grabbed his board and balanced it on his side.

Janey looked into his dark eyes and found herself liking him more. She laughed and let him lead her toward the water.

CHAPTER 6

Janey's skin was as red as a lobster when she got home. She'd been having so much fun with Cody, she completely forgot to put on more sunscreen.

After she showered, she covered her skin with aloe vera cream to make her sunburn feel better. As she put on a pair of baggy blue cotton shorts and matching T-shirt, the phone rang. She went to the nightstand by her bed and picked it up. It was Kyle, asking her where she'd been all day.

Janey sat on her bed and leaned back against the pile of pillows. "Oh, I had some things to do. I went to Santa Monica," she said.

She looked around her room and

listened to Kyle tell her about his day. She liked her room. It had a cool feeling about it with its sea-foam green walls, matching carpet, and white trim.

Kyle talked nonstop about his day at the studio with his father. He told her all about the actors he'd met. Janey murmured "uh-huh" in the right places as he talked. She kept thinking about the beach. She thought again about Cody.

Janey heard Kyle say her name loudly, which made her listen to him again. "What did you say, Kyle? I'm sorry, I didn't hear the last part," she said. She was embarrassed to be caught daydreaming. She yawned.

"Did you just yawn?" Kyle asked.

"Sorry, it's not you. I'm just tired," she answered.

"Well, I'll let you get some sleep," Kyle said. His voice was as cold as ice.

Janey was going to say something, but she heard a click on the other end of the line. Kyle had hung up. She sat up, feeling guilty. Here was Kyle thinking they were a couple and she spent the day with another boy. *We aren't going steady*, she thought. "That's true," she said aloud. She swung her legs off the bed and stood up just as her bedroom door opened.

"Hi. Betty let me in," Ming said.

Janey smiled. She was glad to see her girlfriend. Ming was dressed in a white top and white linen shorts that showed off her bellybutton. Her long black hair was pulled up in a ponytail with a red ribbon. Janey frowned. "Were we supposed to go someplace tonight?" she asked.

Ming looked at her like she thought Janey was crazy. "You know we are. We're supposed to go to the mall and find something to wear to Kyle's party on Friday night."

"I'm sorry. I totally forgot. I went to the beach today and . . . "

Ming interrupted. "I can see. You should have used sunscreen." Ming walked around the room. She picked up stuffed animals, books, and other things to look at, even though she had seen them a hundred times.

"Just let me change and we can go," Janey said. She opened her closet and looked through her clothes.

"So, why did you go to the beach again? You don't really like the beach," Ming said. She sounded like she knew Janey had a special reason for going.

Janey pulled a sundress from a hanger and turned to see her friend staring at her. "Okay, I went to see Cody."

From the look on Ming's face, Janey knew her friend didn't know what she was talking about. "Tim Cody. The guy I introduced you to at the movie theater last night."

Ming's almond-shaped eyes widened with surprise. "The surfer?"

"Yes, the surfer. He was in a contest today, and I went to watch him," Janey said. She shrugged like it was no big deal.

"He's definitely cute," Ming said. "But he's not part of our crowd. Besides, you know what they say about surfers." Ming went to the dressing table and looked at her makeup in the mirror.

"What?" Janey asked. She took off her shorts and pulled on the sundress.

Ming turned back to Janey. "Surfers don't love anything but the waves, and they have lots of girlfriends. You'll be like the flavor of the month."

"Cody isn't like that," Janey said. He had looked at her like she was the only girl in the world. She was pretty sure he wasn't dating anyone else. He even asked for her phone number.

Ming raised one of her pencil-thin eyebrows. "I hope so, for your sake. But what about Kyle? He really likes you. He told Bobby that he was going to give you his letterman's jacket."

Janey felt guilty. Kyle was a nice guy, but there were some things about him she didn't like. She hated his love of money and the way he thought he was better than other people.

"Kyle loves himself too much," Janey argued.

Ming shook her head. "The other night, he seemed to be interested in what you wanted to do."

Janey remembered. Then she told herself, *that was just one time out of many.*

Ming walked to the door and tried to change the subject. "Come on. Let's go shopping," she said. Janey smiled and followed her friend out of the room.

CHAPTER 7

It was almost noon when Janey parked in the Santa Monica Beach parking lot. She hoped she wasn't too late.

As Janey hurried to get to the beach, she became more excited at the thought of seeing Cody again. She laughed out loud. Two joggers smiled at her as they ran past. She smiled back. She twirled in a circle, loving the bright blue of the sky and the smell of the sea.

She didn't see many surfers out in the water or sitting on the beach. She looked around at the people scattered on the sand sunbathing. She was suddenly disappointed. *The contest is over and I've missed him*, she thought.

Then she heard a man's voice through a microphone. "Number 234, fourth place with 425 points, in division two, Matt Lowry."

Janey looked up at the pier. A crowd was standing on the pier near a raised platform. She saw the man with the microphone holding up a ribbon that fluttered in the breeze. Surfboards leaned against the pier's railings. Janey walked over to the stairs that led to the pier as quickly as she could.

As she walked along the pier, passing food stands and amusement rides, Janey tried to find Cody. Finally, she saw him standing off to one side, leaning against the railing, his board propped up next to him.

"Cody!" Janey called out. She waved to him and worked her way through the crowd. Then he was there, grabbing her around her waist. He picked her up and swung her around.

"Whoa! Put me down!" Janey cried.

She was laughing and protesting at the same time.

"I took first prize in my division!" he shouted. His face was bright with happiness.

When Cody set her back on her feet, Janey could still feel herself spinning. Smiling and out of breath, she looked up into his dark eyes. He steadied her with his hands on her shoulders. Cody stepped back from her and smiled. "I'm glad you came."

"I wish I'd been here to see you get your ribbon," Janey said. She suddenly felt very shy.

"Ribbon? I didn't get a little ribbon. I got a trophy." Cody went to his board and squatted down next to a gym bag. He pulled out a small trophy of a golden man on a surfboard.

"That's awesome," Janey said. She was very impressed. "You must be really happy."

Cody shrugged. "Yeah, but I don't

really care about prizes. I just love to surf." He bent back down and put the trophy in the bag.

Janey was about to say something when a pretty blond girl in a bikini walked up. She leaned down over Cody, letting her long hair fall into his face. Janey didn't hear what the girl said, but she heard Cody laugh. Then the girl walked off down the pier.

Cody stood up, holding his bag in one hand. He grabbed his board with the other hand. "Want to get a soda or something?" he asked.

"Sure," Janey said. She carefully kept her eyes from watching the blond girl. She thought of Ming's warning that surfers have lots of girlfriends.

As they walked down the pier, Cody stopped every so often to say hello to a fellow surfer. It seemed like he knew almost everyone on the pier. Finally, they reached the Seahorse Café. Cody found a table for them. He leaned his board against the pier railing.

"Want a burger?" Cody asked.

"That sounds great," Janey said. Suddenly, she was starving.

Cody saw her reach for her purse. "My treat," he said. He went to the counter to order.

In minutes, they were biting into giant burgers. "This is good," Janey said. She put the burger down and licked the dressing off her fingers.

"The best burgers on this side of town," Cody said. He finished his soft drink.

After eating, they began to talk about themselves. They shared information about where they lived, their families, and their interests. Janey wasn't surprised to learn that they liked many of the same things, like the music of the Beach Boys. It was like they were in a world all their own. That's what she thought, until Cody looked at his watch.

"Wow! It's four o'clock. I've gotta go. I'm late," Cody said. He jumped up and grabbed his bag and then his board. "I'm sorry about this. I'll call you later." He smiled at her, then ran down the pier toward the parking lot.

Janey stood up, surprised at the way Cody suddenly left. After throwing away the food containers, she walked across the pier. Below the pier was a stretch of dry sand and then the parking lot.

Janey gasped. She watched Cody slide his board into the back of an old car. The blond girl she'd seen talking to Cody earlier was behind the wheel.

Tears filled Janey's eyes. She watched as Cody jumped into the passenger seat of the car and then drove off.

CHAPTER 8

All Janey could think about the next day was Cody. In the morning, she was very sad. She kept remembering how Cody looked getting into the car with the blond girl. By the afternoon, she had made herself angry. *I wasn't flavor of the month. I was flavor of the minute*, she thought. She pulled open the refrigerator door and stared at the leftovers and other food.

"There's chicken salad in the blue container behind the melon. You want me to make you a sandwich?" Betty asked. She looked up from the flowers she was arranging in a tall crystal vase.

"No, thanks," Janey mumbled. She grabbed an apple and a bottled water.

"Is that all you're going to eat?" Betty asked. She shook her head with disapproval.

"I'm not really hungry," Janey said. Her stomach felt like it was tied in knots. As she left the kitchen, Betty's voice stopped her.

"I forgot to tell you that your friend Ming called," Betty said. "So did a boy named Tim Cody." She carried the vase of roses into the hall and placed them on a table.

"When did they call?" Janey asked. She got excited at the sound of Cody's name.

Betty shrugged. "Early. Before you came down from your room. The Cody boy's number is on the pad in the sunroom."

Janey remembered hearing the phone ring earlier. She thought it was for her parents. Her friends usually called later in the day. She walked into the sunroom and was glad the air conditioner was on. Outside, the afternoon sun made bright spots in the pool. Heat shimmered in the air.

Janey ran her finger over Cody's name and number on the pad. She thought about returning his call. She really wanted to call him, but she couldn't stop thinking about the blond girl's hair falling across Cody's face. Angrily, Janey picked up the phone and dialed Ming's number.

When she heard Ming's voice, Janey told her everything. She even explained how Cody left with another girl. "And don't say 'I told you so,' either," Janey said. There were tears in the corners of her green eyes.

Ming sighed. "Forget him. He doesn't go to our school. And he's not part of our crowd."

Janey frowned. "I don't care if he's not part of our crowd. Our crowd is getting kind of wild, don't you think?"

Ming laughed. "It's called fun,

girlfriend. We're seniors now. Relax. Look, Bobby and I will pick you up at eight for the party," Ming said. After a moment, she thought of something. "Did you tell Kyle?" Ming asked. Her voice sounded worried.

"No, I didn't tell Kyle. I was going to call him," Janey said. She was embarrassed that she forgot all about Kyle and his party.

Again, Ming sighed. "Just forget Tim Cody, okay? Think about Kyle. He's a cool guy, really."

"Yeah," Janey said. When she hung up the phone, Janey looked again at Cody's phone number on the pad. She ripped the page off and put it in the pocket of her shorts. Then she went upstairs to find something to wear to Kyle's party.

CHAPTER 9

When they got to Kyle's house, the party had already started. Loud music blasted from the CD player. It drowned out the roar of the waves.

"This is way too cool!" Bobby shouted. His big bear face grinned like he was in a candy store. Ming held onto his arm. They made their way through groups of kids who were talking, eating, and drinking.

Janey recognized a lot of the kids from her school. She spent several minutes talking to friends she hadn't seen all summer. As she walked past the living room, crowded with more kids, Kyle was suddenly at her side. He put his arm around her shoulders.

"Hey, you are looking really nice tonight," he said. He gave her a big smile. Janey smiled. She was embarrassed, but pleased. She was wearing new black pants and a black top that made her look slim and pretty. Copper-colored bracelets that matched her red hair jingled on her wrists.

"You look nice too, Kyle," Janey said. She noticed the new white tennis shorts and polo shirt he wore. They walked out onto the patio that overlooked the beach.

Bobby and Ming also walked out onto the patio. They kissed for a long time right in front of Janey. Janey stared at her friend. Ming just smiled at her like it was no big deal.

Janey suddenly felt very uncomfortable. She wished she could call her parents to pick her up. They had left that morning for San Diego and wouldn't be back until Sunday night. She knew Betty didn't drive.

As it got later and later, the party got louder. More kids kept arriving. They were kids Janey didn't know. By midnight, every room in the house was crowded. The patio overflowed with kids down to the beach below.

"Who are all these people, Kyle?" Janey yelled. She tried to make herself heard over all the noise.

Kyle shrugged. "Who knows? Somebody must have spread the word about this great party. What's the matter? Aren't you having fun?"

Ming shrieked with laughter. As Janey turned, something cold and sticky splashed on her shoulder. It quickly dripped down her arm and onto her new pants. She looked at Bobby, who was holding a now half-filled cup of soda. Kyle laughed out loud.

Angrier than she'd ever been in her life, Janey pushed her way past Kyle and went down the steps of the patio to the beach.

"Where are you going?" Kyle yelled. His handsome face looked surprised. He was so popular, no one had ever walked away from him.

Janey looked up at him. She realized that things had changed. Her friends liked to have parties and drive fast cars. Janey no longer thought that was fun. She suddenly realized she was not like them at all.

"I'm going away from this party, away from your snobby friends, and away from you!" she shouted.

"Have a nice long walk!" Kyle shouted. He went back to join the party.

Tears filled her eyes as Janey walked to the beach. *Kyle was right,* she thought. *It is a long walk.*

She was miles from her home, without any money. All she knew was that she wasn't going back to the party.

CHAPTER 10

The roar of the ocean grew louder as Janey walked down the dark beach. *I sure showed Kyle by running off like that,* Janey thought. Up ahead, bare light bulbs burned on posts around a small empty parking lot.

She realized she should have walked in the other direction. That's where the houses were, and someone might let her use their phone to call a taxi. It meant walking past Kyle's beach house again.

A car drove into the beach parking lot. Its headlights shined through the darkness. Then the lights went out. A man stepped out of the car. Janey was too far away to see him clearly. She only knew that now she was not alone. She stood perfectly still, holding her breath.

The man started walking across the sand in her direction. Janey turned, ready to run back down the beach. The beam of a flashlight shined in her face. Then the light left her face and shined on the ground. Janey began to run in the darkness.

"Janey! Janey, wait. It's me!" Cody yelled. He jogged the last few yards toward her. He shined the flashlight in his own face.

Janey sighed with relief. "What are you doing out here?" Janey asked.

Cody laughed, a big, warm, and friendly laugh. "Looking for you."

"Me? How did you know I was out here?"

"I work down the road at the Tidewater Restaurant," Cody said. "When I was done, a couple of my buddies came by and said there was a big party down at Kyle Anderson's place on Rider Road. They said it was an open party and anyone could go."

Janey nodded. She remembered how the party had gotten crowded with kids no one knew. "I'll bet your blond girlfriend from the pier won't be happy to hear that," Janey said angrily.

Cody stared at her for a minute, then he laughed. "She isn't my girl-friend. We work together at the restaurant. Sheila gave me a ride because my car was in the shop. So that's why you didn't return my phone calls. You thought Sheila and I were dating."

Janey nodded. She was still angry. "Why didn't you tell me you were going to work? You just left me sitting at that picnic table and ran off. What was I supposed to think?"

Cody cleared his throat and looked out at the ocean. "Well, I was going to tell you, but I thought you wouldn't like me if you knew I worked in a restaurant. I'm not rich like you and all your friends."

"I don't care if you're not rich," Janey said. Joy replaced the anger she had been feeling.

Cody reached out and pulled her close to him. He held her. "I went to the party looking for you," he smiled.

"I went to the party looking for you," Cody smiled.

"Really?" Janey asked.

"Yes," Cody whispered. "I wanted to give you this." He dropped a pink-and-white curved shell in her hand.

"Oh, it's beautiful," Janey said. She remembered it as the shell that disappeared from her hand the day his board banged into her leg. "I love it."

"I love you," Cody said. He leaned down and kissed her. She kissed him back.

Stars twinkled in the sky as the moon cast a golden shadow across the water.